P9-CQF-559

EL CASTILLO MISTERIOSO
MYSTERY CASTLE

Illustrated by Brenda Haw

Adapted from Puzzle Castle by Kathy Gemmell & Nicole Irving

Bilingual editor: Kate Needham
Design adaptation by John Russell

Language consultants:

Esther Lecumberri & Marta Nuñez

Original story by Susannah Leigh

Edited by Gaby Waters
Designed by Paul Greenleaf

Contents

About this book

This book is about a brave knight called Silvia and her adventure at Mystery Castle. The story is in Spanish and English. You can look up the word list on page 23 if you want to check what any Spanish word means. This list also shows you how to say each Spanish word.

Silvia

El Castillo Misterioso

There is a puzzle on every double page. Solve each one and help Silvia on her way. All the Spanish words you need to solve the puzzles are in the word keys (look out for this sign: 🔑). If you get stuck, the answers are on page 22.

La historia The story

El amigo de Silvia, Pablo, vive en el Castillo Misterioso. Le ha escrito esta carta:

Silvia's friend, Pablo, lives in Mystery Castle. He has written her this letter:

Pablo

El Castillo Misterioso	Mystery Castle
Querida Silvia,	Dear Silvia,
Estás invitada esta noche al banquete del castillo.	You are invited to the castle banquet this evening.
Comenzará a las seis.	It will start at six.
Tenemos un pequeño problema.	We have a little problem.
Hay un monstruo en alguna parte de las mazmorras.	There is a monster somewhere in the dungeons.
Tú eres muy, muy, muy valiente.	You are very, very, very brave.
¿Podrías venir antes para encontrar al monstruo?	Can you come early to find the monster?
Tu amigo, Pablo	Your friend, Pablo

Things to look for

When Silvia gets to the castle, she must collect the seven things shown here. They will all help her to find the monster. You will find one of them on each double page, from the moment she sees the castle, until she reaches the dungeons.

el paraguas verde
green umbrella

la superlinterna
super flashlight

los zapatos veloces
run-fast shoes

el escudo anti-monstruo
anti-monster shield

el diccionario del idioma de los monstruos
monster-language dictionary

el casco anti-monstruo
anti-monster helmet

la llave
key

Felipe, the ghost

Mystery Castle is haunted by a friendly ghost, called Felipe. He is hiding on every double page. See if you can spot him.

Tito, the juggler

Tito is working on his juggling for the banquet, but he is not very good at it. He has lost his juggling balls around the castle. There is at least one hiding on every double page. Can you find them?

The juggling balls look like this.

How to sound Spanish

Some Spanish letters sound different. Here are a few tips to help you say them.

You never say h, but the letter j is said like the "h" in "half". Ll is like the "y" in "yes", ñ is like the first "n" in "onion", qu is like the "c" in "cat", u is like the "oo" in "root" and v is like the "b" in "bad". Y is like the "y" in yes, but on its own, it is like the "e" in "me". Z is like the "th" in "this" in north or central Spain, but in southern Spain or South America it is like the "s" in "sat".

The Spanish r is trilled, a little like a dog growling. C and g only sound different when they come before "i" or "e". Then, c is like z, (it sounds like "th" or "s"), and g is like j, (it sounds like "h").

3

El castillo The castle

Silvia sale rápidamente hacia el castillo.
Silvia quickly sets off for the castle.

Dice adiós a sus padres.
She says goodbye to her parents.

En seguida llega al foso del castillo.
Soon she arrives at the castle moat.

Pero ¿qué camino debe tomar para cruzar?
But which route must she take to cross?

El conejo le da la primera indicación.
The rabbit gives her the first direction.

Can you spot the rabbit?
Follow all the directions and find the right
way to cross the moat.

No cruces este puente.

Prohibido el paso.

Adiós.

No cruces este puente.

Gira a la derecha.

Cruza el puente verde.

4

El mapa The map

Silvia encuentra a Pablo a la entrada del castillo. Pablo le da el mapa del castillo.

Silvia finds Pablo outside the castle entrance. Pablo gives her the map of the castle.

"El monstruo está en las mazmorras. Para llegar allí, debes ir al sótano."

"The monster is in the dungeons. To get there, you have to go to the cellar."

"En el camino, debes visitar a cuatro personas."

"On the way, you must visit four people."

"Todo el mundo se está preparando para el banquete. Todos necesitan tu ayuda."

"Everybody is getting ready for the banquet. They all need your help."

Can you match the four people on the list with the rooms where Silvia will find them? She must visit them in order. Which route will she take to the cellar?

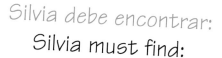

1. Julián, el guardián de los retratos
Julián, the portrait keeper

2. La princesa Florinda
Princess Florinda

3. Martín, el vigía del castillo
Martín, the castle's lookout boy

4. La Señora Pimentón, la cocinera
Mrs. Pimentón, the cook

Key 🔑

la torre de vigía	lookout tower
el ático	attic
el estudio	study
la habitación de ...	...'s bedroom
la galería de retratos	portrait gallery
la entrada	entrance
las mazmorras	dungeons
el salón de los banquetes	banquet hall
la cocina	kitchen
el baño	bathroom
las escaleras	stairs
el sótano	cellar
el garaje	garage
la biblioteca	library

El mapa del castillo Map of the castle

la torre de vigía

el ático

el estudio

la habitación de Florinda

la galería de retratos

la entrada

el salón de los banquetes

la cocina

la habitación de Pablo

la biblioteca

el baño

las escaleras

el garaje

el sótano

las mazmorras

La galería de retratos
The portrait gallery

Silvia visita primero la galería de retratos.
Silvia visits the portrait gallery first.

Julián, el guardián de los retratos, está preocupado.
Julián, the portrait keeper, is worried.

"El tío Santiago va a venir al banquete."
"Uncle Santiago is going to come to the banquet."

"Tengo que encontrarme con él cerca del foso, pero se me ha olvidado cómo es."
"I have to meet him by the moat, but I've forgotten what he looks like."

Which portrait is Uncle Santiago's? There is only one which fits what everyone is saying.

La búsqueda del tesoro
The treasure hunt

Después, Silvia visita a la princesa Florinda.
Next, Silvia visits Princess Florinda.

Está en su habitación. ¡Qué lío!
She is in her bedroom. What a mess!

"¡Silvia, estás aquí!" grita Florinda.
"Here you are, Silvia!" shouts Florinda.

"He perdido el collar, la pulsera, el anillo y la corona."
"I've lost my necklace, my bracelet, my ring and my crown."

Algunas cosas más han desaparecido.
Some other things have disappeared.

Can you find a necklace, bracelet, ring and crown that match? Read the speech bubbles and point to all the other things that are lost.

He perdido la flauta.

He perdido la corneta.

10

11

La torre de vigía The lookout tower

Silvia se despide de la princesa. Sube a la torre de vigía.
La gente ya está llegando para el banquete.

Silvia says goodbye to the princess. She climbs up to the lookout
tower. People are already arriving for the banquet.

Martín, el vigía, no sabe si todo el mundo está invitado.
"Silvia," grita, "¡haz algo!"

Martín, the lookout boy, does not know if everyone is invited.
"Silvia," he cries, "do something!"

**Using Martín's list, can you help Silvia tell him which of
the people in the picture are not invited? What
treatment will they get?**

La lista de Martín

La reina de Vistabella, Violeta: invitada.
La reina de Monteperdido, Marieta: no invitada -
recibirla con estiércol.
La reina de Aguaclara, Alicia: no invitada -
recibirla con sopa de cebolla.
La reina de Rioverde, Raquel: no invitada -
recibirla con mermelada.
La princesa de Monteflorido, Miranda: invitada.
El rey de Requesón, Rodrigo: invitado.
El príncipe de Requesón, Renato, y su perro, Feroz:
no invitados - recibirlos con huevos podridos.

HUEVOS PODRIDOS

ESTIÉRCOL

MERMELADA

SOPA DE CEBOLLA

Key 🗝️

me llamo	my name is	(los) huevos podridos	rotten eggs
vengo de	I come from	(la) sopa de cebolla	onion soup
la lista de ...	...'s list	(la) mermelada	jam
el rey de	the king of	invitado/a	invited
la reina de	the queen of	no invitado/a(s)	not invited
el príncipe de	the prince of	recibirlo/a	welcome him/her
la princesa de	the princess of	recibirlos	welcome them
su perro	his dog	con	with
(el) estiércol	dung	y	and

En la cocina In the kitchen

Después, Silvia va a la cocina.
Next, Silvia goes to the kitchen.

La Señora Pimentón parece preocupada.
Mrs. Pimentón looks worried.

"¿Qué pasa?" pregunta Silvia.
"What's the matter?" asks Silvia.

"Tengo que hacer un gran pastel para el banquete, pero no encuentro los ingredientes".
"I must make a big cake for the banquet, but I can't find the ingredients."

"Sé que están aquí, por alguna parte."
"I know they're here somewhere".

Can you spot all the ingredients Mrs. Pimentón is looking for somewhere in the kitchen?

AZÚCAR

AGUA   MIEL

HARINA

Key 🔑

estoy buscando	I am looking for
un	one OR a
dos	two
tres	three
cuatro	four
un tarro de	a pot of
(la) miel	honey
(los) huevos frescos	fresh eggs
(los) panes	loaves of bread
(el) limón	lemon
(las) ciruelas rojas	red plums
(el) azúcar	sugar
(la) harina	flour
(el) queso	cheese
(la) leche	milk
(el) agua	water
y	and

Estoy buscando dos ciruelas rojas, un tarro de miel, tres huevos frescos, cuatro panes y un limón.

QUESO

LECHE

15

El sótano The cellar

Silvia sale de la cocina y baja al sótano.
Silvia leaves the kitchen and goes down to the cellar.

"Oh," dice, mirando el mapa, "aquí hay muchas puertas."
"Oh," she says, looking at the map, "there are lots of doors here."

"¿Cuál es la puerta para ir a las mazmorras?"
"Which is the right door to get to the dungeons?"

Por suerte, los animales que viven en la bodega dicen siempre la verdad.
Luckily, the animals who live in the cellar always tell the truth.

Can you work out from what all the animals are saying which door Silvia should take?

No abras la puerta amarilla.

No abras la puerta anaranjada.

En las mazmorras **In the dungeons**

Por fin, Silvia entra en las mazmorras.
At last, Silvia enters the dungeons.

Oye voces extrañas.
She hears strange voices.

"Pablo ya me había avisado," dice.
"Pablo warned me about this," she says.

"Los animales que viven aquí no dicen nunca la verdad."
"The animals who live here never tell the truth."

"Debo hacer siempre lo contrario de lo que dicen."
"I must always do the opposite of what they say."

Read what the animals are saying. Can you give Silvia the correct directions to find the monster?

Did you remember to look for all Silvia's useful equipment? Look back to page 3 to check you have found everything.

Key

abre	open
no abras	do not open
la puerta	the door
gira	turn
no gires	do not turn
a la derecha	to the right
a la izquierda	to the left
¿cómo te llamas?	what is your name?
me llamo	my name is
he perdido a	I have lost
mi mamá	my mother
la llave	the key

El banquete The banquet

Es la hora del banquete.
It is time for the banquet.

Silvia y el monstruito se están divirtiendo mucho. ¿Los puedes ver?
Silvia and the little monster are having a great time. Can you see them?

Todo el mundo está muy contento, pero algunos invitados han perdido cosas.
Everyone is very happy, but some guests have lost things.

Silvia no puede ayudar a todos.
Silvia cannot help them all.

Can you spot all the things that people are looking for? Who will be especially pleased to see the little monster?

¿Dónde está mi hijo?

¿Dónde está mi osito?

¿Dónde está el cerdo?

¿Dónde está la sopa verde?

¿Dónde está el pan?

¿Dónde está la puerta?

Answers

Pages 4-5

The route Silvia should take is shown in red.

Pages 6-7

Silvia's route will take her to: Julián in la galería de retratos (the portrait gallery), Florinda in la habitación de Florinda (Florinda's bedroom), Martín in la torre de vigía (the lookout tower) and Mrs. Pimentón in la cocina (the kitchen).

Pages 8-9

This is Uncle Santiago's portrait.

Pages 10-11

Florinda's matching jewels are circled in red. All the other missing objects are circled in blue.

Pages 12-13

Renato, el príncipe de Requesón and his dog, Feroz are not invited. They will get the rotten egg treatment.

Pages 14-15

The missing ingredients are circled in red.

Pages 16-17

Silvia should go through this door.

Pages 18-19

Here are the correct directions: Gira a la izquierda. Gira a la derecha. Gira a la izquierda. Gira la llave. Abre la puerta.

The monster is crying because he has lost his mother.

Pages 20-21

All the things that people are looking for are circled in red. Boris's mother is especially pleased to see him. Here she is.

Did you spot everything?

Pages	Juggling balls	Equipment to find
4-5	one	anti-monster shield
6-7	one	key
8-9	three	super flashlight
10-11	four	run-fast shoes
12-13	two	green umbrella
14-15	four	monster-language dictionary
16-17	two	anti-monster helmet
18-19	one	none here!
20-21	nineteen	none here!

Did you remember to look out for Felipe the ghost? Look back and find him on every double page.

Word list and pronunciation guide

Here is a list of all the Spanish words and phrases used in this book. All the naming words (nouns) have el, la, los or las before them. These all mean "the". Spanish nouns are either masculine or feminine. You use el and los with masculine nouns, and la and las with feminine nouns. When you see los or las, it means the noun is plural (more than one).

Spanish describing words (adjectives) ending in o change to a when they describe feminine nouns. Here, the masculine version is written first, followed by /a, for example rojo/a (red). When an adjective describes a plural noun, it usually has an s after the o or a.

Each Spanish word in this list has its pronunciation shown after it (in letters like this). Read these letters as if they were English words. The ones that are underlined should be said slightly louder than the rest. In South America or southern Spain, the "th" sound shown here is pronounced as "ss". For more about how to say Spanish words see page 3.

a	a	to
abre	abray	open
adiós	adeeyoss	goodbye
el agua	el agwa	water
al	al	to the
algo	algo	something
alguna parte	algoona parte	somewhere
algunos/as	algoonoss/ass	some
allí	alyee	there
amarillo/a	amareelyo/a	yellow
el amigo	el ameego	friend
anaranjado/a	anaranhado/a	orange
el anillo	el aneelyo	ring
los animales	loss aneemaless	animals
antes	antess	before
aquí	akee	here
el ático	el ateeko	attic
avisado	abeessado	warned
la ayuda	la ayooda	help
ayudar	ayoodar	to help
el azúcar	el athookar	sugar
azul	athool	blue
baja	baha	(he/she) goes down
el baño	el banyo	bathroom
el banquete	el banketay	banquet
la barba	la barba	beard
el bastón	el baston	walking stick
la biblioteca	la beeblee-oteka	library
bienvenido/a	bee-enbeneedo/a	welcome
la bodega	la bodega	cellar
buscando	boosskando	looking for
la búsqueda	la boosskeda	hunt OR search
el caballo	el kabalyo	horse
el camino	el kameeno	path OR way
el casco	el kassko	helmet
el castillo	el kassteelyo	castle
la cebolla	la thebolya	onion
cerca	thairka	near OR by
el cerdo	el thairdo	pig
cinco	theenko	five
las ciruelas	lass theerwellass	plums
la cocina	la kotheena	kitchen
la cocinera	la kotheenaira	cook
el collar	el kolyar	necklace
comenzar	komenthar	to begin
comenzará	komenthara	(he/she/it) will begin
¿cómo?	komo	what? OR how?
¿cómo es?	komo ess	what's he/she like?
¿cómo te llamas?	komo tay lyamass	what's your name?
con	kon	with
el conejo	el koneho	rabbit
contento/a	kontento/a	happy
el contrario	el kontrareeyo	the opposite
la corneta	la korneta	horn
la corona	la korona	crown
las cosas	lass kossass	things
cruza	krootha	cross
cuál	kwal	which
cuatro	kwatro	four
da	da	(he/she) gives
de	day	of OR from
debe	debay	(he/she) must
debes	debess	you must
debo	debo	I must
del	del	of the
la derecha	la derecha	right
desaparecido/a	dessaparetheedo/a	disappeared
después	desspwess	next OR after
el diccionario	el deektheeyonareeyo	dictionary
dice	deethay	(he/she) says OR tells
dicen	deethen	(they) say OR tell
dónde	donday	where
dos	doss	two
el	el	the
él	el	he OR him
en	en	in
encontrar	enkontrar	to find OR to meet
encuentra	enkwentra	(he/she) finds
en seguida	en segeeda	right away OR soon
entra	entra	(he/she) enters
la entrada	la entrada	entrance
eres	eress	you are
es	ess	(he/she/it) is
las escaleras	lass esskalairass	stairs

23

Spanish	Pronunciation	English
escrito	esskreeto	written
el escudo	el esskoodo	shield
esta, este	essta, esstay	this
está	essta	(he/she) is
están	esstan	(they) are
estás	esstass	you are
el estiércol	el essteeyairkol	dung
estoy	esstoy	I am
el estudio	el esstoodeeyo	study
extrañas	extranyass	strange
feroz	feroth	fierce
la flauta	la fla-ota	recorder OR flute
las flores	las floress	flowers
el foso	el fosso	moat OR ditch
fresco/a	fressko/a	fresh
las gafas	lass gafass	glasses
la galería	la galereeya	gallery
el garaje	el garahay	garage
el gato	el gato	cat
la gente	la hentay	people
gira	heera	turn
gran, grande	gran, granday	big OR large
grita	greeta	(he/she) shouts
el guardián	el gwardeeyan	keeper OR guard
ha ...	a ...	(he/she) has ...
había	abeeya	there was OR (he/she) had ...
la habitación	la abeetatheeyon	room
hacer	athair	to make OR to do
hacia	atheeya	toward
han ...	an ...	(they) have ...
la harina	la areena	flour
hay	eye	there is OR there are
haz algo	ath algo	do something
he ...	ay ...	I have ...
el hijo	el eeho	son OR child
la historia	la eestoreeya	story
hola	ola	hello
la hora	la ora	hour OR time
los huevos	loss webboss	eggs
el idioma	el eedeeyoma	language
la indicación	la eendeekatheeyon	direction
los ingredientes	loss eengredeeyentess	ingredients
invitado/a	eenbeetado/a	invited
los invitados	loss eenbeetadoss	guests
ir	eer	to go
la izquierda	la eethkeeyairda	left
la, las	la, lass	the OR her, them
le	lay	to him OR to her
la leche	la lechay	milk
el limón	el leemon	lemon
la lista	la leessta	list
la llave	la lyabay	key
llegando	lyegando	arriving
llegar	lyegar	to arrive
los	loss	the OR them
la mamá	la mama	mother
el mapa	el mapa	map
más	mass	more
las mazmorras	lass mathmorrass	dungeons
me llamo	may lyamo	my name is
la mermelada	la mairmelada	jam
mi, mis	mee, meess	my
la miel	la meeyell	honey
mira	meera	(he/she) looks (at)
mirando	meerando	looking at
misterioso	meesstereeyosso	mysterious
el monstruito	el monsstrweeto	little monster
el monstruo	el monsstrwo	monster
mucho/a	moocho/a	much OR many
muy	mooy	very
necesitan	nethesseetan	(they) need
negro/a	negro/a	black
no abras	no abrass	do not open
no cruces	no kroothess	do not cross
no encuentro	no enkwentro	I cannot find
no gires	no heeress	do not turn
no invitado/a	no eenbeetado/a	not invited
no puede	no pweday	(he/she) cannot
no tiene	no teeyenay	(he/she/it) does not have
la noche	la nochay	night
el número	el noomero	number
nunca	noonka	never
el osito	el osseeto	little bear
oye	oyay	(he/she) hears
los padres	loss padress	parents
el pan	el pan	bread
los panes	loss paness	loaves of bread
para	para	for OR to
el paraguas	el paragwass	umbrella
parece	parethay	(it/he/she) seems
el pastel	el pastel	cake
el pelo	el pelo	hair
pequeño/a	pekenyo/a	small OR little
perdido/a	pairdeedo/a	lost
pero	pero	but
el perro	el perro	dog
las personas	lass pairssonass	people
el pimentón	el peementon	red pepper
¿podrías ...?	podreeyass	could you...?
podrido/a	podreedo/a	rotten
por fin	por feen	at last
por suerte	por swairtay	luckily
pregunta	pregoonta	(he/she) asks
preocupado/a	prayokoopado/a	worried
primero/a	preemairo/a	first
la princesa	la preenthessa	princess